THE *Princess* IN **BLACK**
and the MERMAID PRINCESS

THE Princess IN BLACK

and the MERMAID PRINCESS

Shannon Hale & Dean Hale

illustrated by
LeUyen Pham

CANDLEWICK PRESS

Text copyright © 2022 by Shannon and Dean Hale
Illustrations copyright © 2022 by LeUyen Pham

First edition 2022

Library of Congress Catalog Card Number pending
ISBN 978-1-5362-0977-8

21 22 23 24 25 26 LEO 10 9 8 7 6 5 4 3 2 1

Printed in Heshan, Guangdong, China

This book was typeset in LTC Kennerley Pro.
The illustrations were done in watercolor and ink.

Candlewick Press
99 Dover Street
Somerville, Massachusetts 02144

www.candlewick.com

For our beloved Grandpa Bush,
deep-sea explorer at heart
SH and DH

To Indira,
the Mermaid Princess
LP

Chapter 1

The Princess in Black was sailing
on a boat named the *Lively Turnip*.
The sun was sparkling on the waves.
The breeze was salty and cool. She
was having a princess hero playdate
with her two best pals. It was sure
to be an exciting day.

"So kind of Princess Sneezewort to lend us her royal boat," said the Princess in Black.

"Yes, she hoped we could use it to look out for monsters," said the Princess in Blankets.

"Monsters?" The Goat Avenger stood up. "Are there *sea* monsters?"

"Indeed." The Princess in Blankets narrowed her eyes and whispered into the breeze, "At least one . . ."

"That's right," said the Princess in Black. "One time I battled a sea monster on the beach."

"A huge sea monster. A *colossal* sea monster!" The Princess in Blankets shrugged. "Um, Princess Sneezewort told me about it."

A sea monster would certainly make the day exciting. But what the Princess in Black longed to see was a mermaid. People said mermaids didn't exist, but she hoped they did. She believed.

The water gurgled near the boat. The sea sloshed against its side. And suddenly, something sprang from the waves.

"Monster!" cried the Princess in Blankets.

"Mermaid!" yelled the Princess in Black.

"Goat!" shouted the Goat Avenger. "Wait, it's probably not a goat. Sorry."

The Something swam away. The Princess in Black didn't see it clearly, but she hoped . . .

"PURSUE THE CREATURE!" the Princess in Blankets shouted.

The princesses opened the sail, and the Goat Avenger steered the boat.

They chased the Something over waves. Around rocks. Past a very lazy octopus . . .

And finally found it resting on a little island.

"That's definitely not a goat," said the Goat Avenger.

"And it isn't a monster," said the Princess in Blankets.

"eeeeeEEEEEEEEE!" the Princess in Black squealed with excitement.

Because it *was* a mermaid.

A mermaid princess!

Chapter 2

The Princess in Black was still "eeeeeEEEE"-ing. And hopping around. And smiling so hard, she couldn't remember how to stop.

A mermaid. A real live mermaid!

"Hi," said the mermaid.

"SHE SAID HI!" said the Princess in Black, dance-hopping.

"Hello, mermaid who definitely isn't a monster. I'm the Princess in Blankets, and these are my friends the Princess in Black—"

"Hi!" said the Princess in Black, waving with both hands.

"—and the Goat Avenger."

"I'm Princess Posy," said the mermaid. She smiled, but her eyes looked
sad. The Princess in Black gasped.

"Oh no, something is wrong! Can
we help you?"

With the tip of her pinkie, the mermaid petted a crab on its tiny head.

"I wish someone could. I'm afraid I'm going to fail at the most important job of a princess."

"What is the most important job of a princess?" asked the Goat Avenger.

"Protecting her kingdom," said the three princesses at the same time.

"Ah," said the Goat Avenger.

"A trench leading to Kraken Land cracked open in the capricorn pasture," said Princess Posy.

"Huh?" said the Goat Avenger.

"I can guess what a kraken is," said the Princess in Black. "But what are capricorns?"

"Sea goats," said the mermaid. "They're just the cutest."

The Goat Avenger stared. "*Sea* goats?"

"What if a kraken comes out of the trench?" said Princess Posy. "I don't know how to stop a kraken from eating the cute little capricorns."

"Princess Posy, we just might be able to help," said the Princess in Blankets.

"Yes, yes, yes!" The Princess in Black was still hopping. "After all, we do have experience protecting goats. Land goats, that is."

Princess Posy looked up at them, and her eyes went wide. "Wait . . . you have masks. And capes too. You're heroes!"

"That's right," said the Goat Avenger. He put his fists on his hips.

"Oh, kind heroes," said Princess Posy, "could you, maybe, come to my kingdom and—"

"YES!" shouted the Princess in Black. "AND SORRY FOR INTERRUPTING BUT YES WE WILL ABSOLUTELY GO TO YOUR MERMAID KINGDOM."

Chapter 3

The boat had diving gear, including fishbowl helmets for non-mermaid heads. The heroes got dressed up. And they dove into the water.

The Princess in Black *ooh*-ed at the jewel-blue world beneath the waves.

She swam beside the mermaid through forests of kelp. Around a lazy octopus. Past a cheeky sea snail. And into the mermaid kingdom. She squealed so much, her helmet fogged up.

"Hello," Princess Posy said whenever she passed a fish. They listened to her, and they followed her. She had a trail of sparkly, finny friends.

SEA TREATS

"Over there are some sea cows,"
said Princess Posy.

"Wow! We have land cows," said
the Princess in Black.

"And there's the underwater volcano I made for a science fair."

"We have science fairs too!" said the Princess in Black.

"Really? And here's my faithful narwhal, Krimpledance."

The Princess in Black spun around excitedly. A narwhal! Named Krimpledance! "Back home there's a unicorn named Frimplepants!"

"A real live unicorn?" said Princess Posy. "I didn't think that unicorns existed! But I hoped . . ."

They swam to a coral castle. At the front, a mermaid was waiting.

"That's Duchess Squidflower," Princess Posy said sadly.

"Princess Posy," said Duchess Squidflower, "I am now storing my trident collection in the tower room."

As Duchess Squidflower swam away, Princess Posy whispered, "But the tower room was my bedroom."

"That didn't seem very nice," said the Princess in Black.

"No," said Princess Posy. "But—"

A frazzled merman interrupted.

"Princess Posy! Some merpeople are using sponges to wash their dishes!"

"Is that bad?" asked the Princess in Blankets.

"The sponges don't like it very much," said Princess Posy.

"What shall we do?" asked the merman.

"I'm not sure," said Princess Posy. "I'll have to think about it."

"Wow," said the Goat Avenger. "Being a princess is hard work."

"It is," said the three princesses.

Princess Posy sighed. "Kingdom management takes all my time. I wish I could play more. Swing on kelp trees. Ride Krimpledance. Bake cakes. But there are always so many problems to solve. Like Duchess Squidflower taking over rooms. And the sponge situation."

"Have you tried speaking up?" asked the Princess in Blankets.

"Not really," said Posy. "I'm a princess, and princesses are supposed to be nice."

Princess Posy showed them the reminder card she kept with her.

NICE TIPS

1. Talk to lonely creatures.
2. Don't make fun of anyone.
3. Protect your friends from things that might eat them.

"Those are great!" said the Princess in Blankets. "I carry a card too."

PRINCESS TIPS
1. Speak up!

"There are more tips," said the Princess in Blankets. "But number one is so big, it took up all the space."

Chapter 4

Princess Posy led the heroes to the kelp pasture. Her excitement began to cool. Nervousness bubbled up instead. What if the heroes couldn't help her after all? What if she couldn't protect her kingdom?

In the pasture, the sea goats were calm and happy, grazing on seaweed. They snuffled wetly. They snoozed bubbily.

"eeeeeEEEEEEEEEE!" squealed the Goat Avenger. He was very excited.

A merboy in a kelp vest and a shell hat was standing guard—or *floating* guard.

"This is Guff," said Princess Posy. "Guff the capricorn boy."

"I LOVE GOATS!" shouted the Goat Avenger.

"I've always wondered," said Guff, "do land goats love bedtime stories as much as sea goats do?"

"Absolutely!" said the Goat Avenger. "Do yours love hot chocolate?"

"Yes," said Guff, "but we call it wet chocolate!"

Princess Posy swam to the edge
of a huge, dark trench. The tips of
her tail went cold.

"There it is," she said, "the hole
to Kraken Land."

The Princess in Blankets peered
into the darkness.

"Yep," she said, "I'm pretty sure
I know what's down there."

Chapter 5

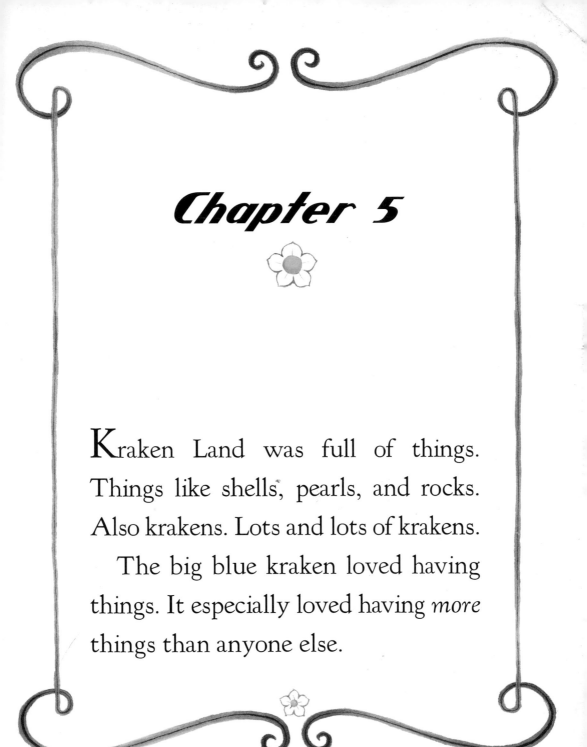

Kraken Land was full of things. Things like shells, pearls, and rocks. Also krakens. Lots and lots of krakens.

The big blue kraken loved having things. It especially loved having *more* things than anyone else.

Feeling very greedy today, it decided to go on a Taking Trek. A Taking Trek is when the big blue kraken would trek around and take whatever it wanted.

Some squid krakens were painting with ink.

"MINE," the big blue kraken gurgled, taking their ink.

Some oyster krakens were playing catch with pearls.

"MINE," the big blue kraken roared, taking their pearls.

It eyed a starfish kraken.

"MINE," the big blue kraken screeched.

The starfish kraken was confused. It didn't have anything to take.

So the big blue kraken took the starfish kraken.

Now the big blue kraken had all the things. But it still wanted more.

There was a hole in the ceiling of Kraken Land. A smell swam through the hole. A smell of sea goats. Plump sea goats. Scaly sea goats. Delicious sea goats.

"MINE . . ." muttered the big blue kraken.

Chapter 6

There was a rumble, a grumble, and a crack. A big blue kraken shoved its way out of the trench.

"EAT SEA GOATS," it gurgled.

"Yep," said the Princess in Blankets. "That's what I thought."

"Don't worry, Princess Posy. We've got this!" The Princess in Black leaped a mighty leap. The leap was so mighty, she floated right over the kraken.

The Goat Avenger struck a battle pose. "Back, beast!" he shouted mightily. He shouted so mightily that it echoed inside his helmet. His ears hurt.

"You may not eat the sea goats!" said the Princess in Blankets. She kicked a mighty kick. The kick was so mighty, it turned her upside down.

They had battled monsters in a goat pasture. And in a park. And even at a science fair. But battling monsters underwater seemed impossible.

Chapter 7

Princess Posy's new friends were fighting the kraken!

Or were they? It was hard to tell. The Princess in Black was floating by. The Goat Avenger was tangled in kelp. The Princess in Blankets was upside-down.

"Hello," said the Princess in Blankets from above her.

"Hi," said Princess Posy. "Are you fighting the kraken?"

"Well, we are trying."

The kraken poked the Princess in Black. She started to float away.

The Goat Avenger freed himself from the kelp. He raced toward the kraken as fast as he could! Which wasn't very fast. It was hard running in water. The cheeky sea snail was going faster.

The Princess in Blankets paddled at the water, trying to turn right-side up. Princess Posy helped.

"You are so fast in the water!" said the Princess in Blankets. "And I noticed that the fish all listen to you. If you speak up, maybe the kraken will listen too!"

Princess Posy consulted her Nice card. "Is speaking up nice?"

"Yes, I think speaking up is very nice," said the Princess in Blankets.

"And I think the capricorns and
the sponges would agree."

The kraken had wrapped the two heroes in a bow of seaweed. Now it turned its glowing eyes on the sea goats. They shivered.

"Wait!" said Princess Posy. "BEHAVE, BEAST!"

"NO!" said the kraken. "MINE!"

As the Princess in Blankets drifted away, she called back, "Remember, it's nice to protect your friends from things that might eat them!"

Princess Posy didn't feel nervous anymore. Having friends on her side definitely helped.

She swam to the kraken. "You may not eat the sea goats!"

"EAT SEA GOATS!" said the kraken again.

So the mermaid princess and the big blue kraken waged battle.

KELP-TREE SWING!❀

KRIMPLE-DANCE RAM!❀

The kraken crawled back into Kraken Land.

"It went home!" said Princess Posy.

"They always do," said the Princess in Blankets.

"Eventually," added the Goat Avenger.

Chapter 8

The Princess in Black tapped her helmet. "I think I'm getting low on air."

"Me too," said the Goat Avenger.

"Thank you so much for your help," said Princess Posy. "I think I can handle it now."

"Aw," said the Princess in Black. "But I love it here!"

"Please visit again," said Princess Posy.

The three heroes floated up with the bubbles. They waved and called down, "We will!"

Princess Posy swam back to her castle. The capricorns were safe. Her sparkly fish friends followed her like a trail of glitter. She felt amazing. She felt powerful.

She felt like a princess.

Duchess Squidflower was waiting. "By the way, I am turning your play-room into a shrimp farm," she said.

"I'm going to use these sponges for dishwashing!" shouted a merman.

"We'd really rather you not," said the sponges.

So Princess Posy waged kingdom management.

RULES:
1. SPONGES ARE FRIENDS, NOT CLEANING SUPPLIES.
2. TRY CLEANING WITH WATER INSTEAD. (THERE'S LOTS!)
3. MAKE A SPONGE FRIEND TODAY!

RULE-MAKING ROMP!

In the end, the kingdom got managed.
It always did. Eventually.

Chapter 9

The Princess in Black bobbed to the surface. Then the Princess in Blankets. And at last the Goat Avenger. They took off their helmets and took a big breath. Mermaids! Sea goats! Narwhals! A cheeky sea snail! It had been the most exciting playdate ever.

"We saw everything *except* a sea monster," said the Princess in Blankets.

"The kraken was kind of a sea monster," said the Goat Avenger.

"Yes, the kraken was good," said the Princess in Blankets. "But I felt sure we would find the huge sea monster.

The *colossal* sea monster. The one with the long neck and tail."

The Princess in Black squinted up. The sun was high. "We don't have to go home yet. We still have time to play."

The water rumbled. Bubbles gurgled around them.

"That wasn't me," said the Goat Avenger.

A sea monster head peeked out of the water.

"PLAY?" it asked.

The Princess in Blankets nodded.
"Play," she said.

"YAY!" said the sea monster.

The hero pals climbed its head. They slid down its neck. They dove off its back and splashed in the salty sea. The sea monster grinned.

It was huge. It was colossal. It was so big, there was plenty of room when more friends came to play. A mermaid princess. A narwhal named Krimpledance. A herd of happy sponges. And one extremely cheeky sea snail.